Bae Min Seo the 2nd Anthologies

詩作하는 旅者
始作하는 女子

A traveller who writes a poem   A lady who begins again

편저 · 사진 **배 민 서**
Compilation · Photo **Bae Min Seo**

이화문화출판사

시작詩作하는 여자旅者

시작始作하는 여자女子

인 쇄 일 | 2015년 11월 11일
발 행 일 | 2015년 11월 15일
지 은 이 | 배 민 서
사 　 진 | 배 민 서
번 　 역 | 윤 명 수
발 행 처 | 이화문화출판사
　　　　　서울시 종로구 사직로 10길 17(내자동)
　　　　　02-738-9880 (대표전화)
　　　　　02-732-7091~3 (구입문의)
　　　　　02-725-9887 (팩스)
　　　　　www.makebook.net
I S B N | 979-11-5547-189-0 03800
정 　 가 | 12,000원

詩作하는 旅者 始作하는 女子

서 문

　시작하는 순간의 기대와 짜릿함에 대해 생각한다. 태어
나 자라고, 자녀가 성장하여 성인이 되어가는 동안 우리
땅, 우리 하늘을 보며 살아왔다.

　언제 찾아도 가슴을 시원하게 틔워주는 바다는 아버지의
품이었다.

　이번 시집을 준비하며 순간순간 가슴이 벅차오르는 것
은, 또 다른 나의 발견을 위한 시작점에서 작품집을 준비하
고, 우리 산야를 음미하며, 사진이라는 기록을 담았기 때문
이다.

　마라톤 선수가 출발선에서 총성을 기다리는 긴장감이 이
러하리라 짐작된다.

　마라톤 전 구간을 완주하려면 어느 구간은 전력질주를
해야 하고, 어느 구간은 체력을 보충해야 하고, 때로는 경
쟁자도 견제해야 하듯, 우리 삶 역시 마찬가지가 아닌가 싶
다. 좋은 기록을 내기 위해 힘을 조절하는 구간은 스스로
의 결정에 달려있고, 무엇보다 자신의 체력을 믿어야만 가
능한 일이다.

이번 시집 출간과 새로운 선택이 나의 마라톤 코스에서 중요한 전환점이 되어지길 기대하며 나다운 시작(詩作), 나다운 시작(始作)을 하려 한다.

제 몸이 익어가는 아픔을 견디고 낙엽이 되어 떨어져 새 생명을 자라게 하는 들판을 바라보며 진정 우리가 고뇌해야 할 섭리가 무엇인지를 생각하고, 작가의 언어로 찾은 해답이 단 한 사람의 영혼에라도 바람으로 스미기를 바라며, 소소한 일상을 담은 이 책이 발간되기 까지 여러 힘든 과정을 함께해 주신 이화문화출판사와 늘 따뜻한 시선으로 격려해 주시는 바탕시동인 회원님들께 감사를 전하며, 나의 의미이고 힘의 원천인 예슬이에게 고맙다는 말과 사랑한다는 말을 전한다. 모두가 잠든 밤, 그윽한 가로등 아래, 단풍잎의 속삭임이 정겹다.

2015. 11. 배 민 서

Preface

I think about expectation and thrill in the starting moment. I have lived a life looking at our earth and our sky while my offspring was born and grown into an adult. The sea which helped revitalize the heart was my father's bosom at any time.

I was filled with emotion every moment preparing collected poems this time, because I prepared anthologies at the starting point to find another 'self' and appreciate our fields and mountain

The tension of marathoner waiting for a starting signal at the starting line will be probably as you have imagined.

To run the whole course of marathon, you should sprint at a certain place and compensate physical power at any section. Sometime you should keep in check your rivals. Similarly, our life resembled it. To better your record, the section of controlling your force is only rest on you. It is possible that you must depend upon your physical power.

The publication of this anthologies and new selection will be a crucial turning point in my marathon course, I expect.

I am intended to write poems and start again corresponding to me.

Looking at the fields which endures the pain ripening their body and falls into the leaves to make a new life. I think the providence to be anguished and the answer found in author's words will be penetrated into even only one person's soul, I hope.

Until this book with a trivial daily lives is published, many assistants were there. More than anything else, I thank Ewha publisiner and Batang poetry members for encouraging with a warm eyes.

And I want to say to Yeseul, my daughter of 'my meaning and the source of power', "Thank you and I love you!"

Everyone fell asleep at this night. Under the secluded streetlight, the whisper of maple leaf is affectionate.

2015. 11. Bae Min Seo

목 차

계절이 주는 쉼
The resting from the season / 13

대지의 축복
The blessing of the earth / 35

계절이 주는 쉼

The resting from the season

詩作하는 旅者 始作하는 女子

파랑새를 띄워 보낸 저 너머
저벅저벅 다가오는 약속의 시간
두려움이란 놈은 언제나
자신감을 앞서 걷는다

독백만이 걸음을 재촉한다
꽃으로 대답하는 한 줄기 칡넝쿨
아무 때고 반겨주는 해묵은 갈색 의자
힘든 하루를 삼켜 버리고
피를 토하는 붉은 노을
심장에 새겨 두고
앞선 두려움 제쳐 걷는다

보내는 이 없음에.

A traveller who writes a poem
A lady who begins again

A blue bird sent there beyond
time of promise approaching
with a heavy footstep
a fellow of fear precedes a confidence

Only monologue quickens the steps
a stalk of an arrowroot bine
answering as a flower
an age−old brown chair welcomes anytime
swallowing the laborious day
a red dusk shedding the blood
being inscribed in the heart
and then walks prior to the fear

Now that there isn't a sender.

일출

당찬 오름
파도의 연주
하루의 서막이다

두 둥
대지가 깨어난다.

A sunrise

A stately rising
performance of the wave
the prelude of a day

tee–dum–dum
the earth is awakened.

관계

나는 매일 나에게 묻는다
오랫동안 관계가 지속되기 위해
너는 무엇을 할 수 있냐고

오해는 너와 나 서로의 사이를 멀어지게 한다
그러나
이해는 너와 나 서로의 사이를 성장하게 한다

가끔
내 가슴은 무너진다
그러나 다시 일어선다

언제나처럼.

Relationship

I ask a question of myself everyday
What can you do to remain the relation
for a long time

Misunderstanding is loss of relationship
Between you and me each other
But
Understanding is to develop the growth
of relationship
between you and me each other

Sometimes
My heart is broken
But I get up again

As usual.

가을의 일탈

북적이는 까페
창가에 앉는다

삼 삼 오 오
하늘을 낙엽을
길가에 구르는 도토리를 음미한다

망고 스무디 한 잔 치즈 케잌 한 조각
무리 속에 홀로 노래하는 나만의 이어폰

일탈이다.

The deviance of an autumn

A bustling cafe
I sit by the window

By twos and threes
Heaven and fallen leaves
I appreciate an acorn rolling in the street

mango, a cup of smoody
cheese, a piece of cake
My own earphone singing alone in groups

It's a deviance.

계절이 주는 쉼

가끔은 일상적인 것들이
특별한 언어로 다가온다
위안
그리움
애수
그리고

이 모두를 베개 삼아 널브러져 익어가는
고독한 바램.

The resting from the season

Sometimes
a daily things approach
as a special language
consolation
yearning
pathos
and

A solitary wish maturing widely
resting the head on all these things

나답게 그리고 우리

오늘이 있어
내일
기억을 더듬을 수 있겠지

그 날엔
참 잘했다 말할 수 있게

할 수 있는
해야 할
하고 싶은 것을 위해
남아 있는 심장 한 조각마저
태우는 오늘

바로 나
그리고 너
친구라는 이름으로.

I look more and We

As there is a today
tomorrow,
I can feel about for my memory

On that day
You could say that " Well done!"
to be able to
to have to
'burning today' a piece of heart
left to do what you want to do

Oh, it's me
and you
In the name of friend.

너에게로 가는 이월

햇살이 창 열어
단장시키는 이월
부끄러움 앞세워 장식하는 뜰
이월의 웨딩드레스
꽃잎으로 날리는 이월의 눈
아버지의 가녀린 미소에
눈물은 진주가 된다

어쩌란 말인가
갈 수도
가지 않을 수도 없다
이월도
웨딩드레스도.

February coming to you

Sunshine opens the window
and decorates February
a garden of ornament
preceding the shame
wedding dress of February
February's snow scattering the petals

Father's slim smile
tears becomes a pearl
Now, what do I do?
I can go or I can't go, either
February and wedding dress, too.

노을이 아름답다

사람도 하늘도
노을이 아름답기는 매한가지
마지막 정열
마지막 아름다움
마지막 사랑
마지막 회한
마지막 희망

또 다른 시작을 담아내는 이유로.

The dusk is beautiful

Both man and the sky
are beautiful at shut of day

the last passion
the last beauty
the last love
the last regret
the last hope

In the cause of including another start.

눈동자의 언어

기쁨을 말할 때 반짝이는 별
슬픔을 말할 때 흔들리는 촛불
사랑을 말할 때 잔잔한 호수
이별을 말할 때 눈 내리는 바다가 된다

너의 눈 속에
내 언어는
개기일식을 마친 찬란한 태양.

The language of the pupil

When you say pleasure, it is a glittering star
when you say sadness, it is a shaking candlelight
when you say love, it is a guiet lake
when you say separation, it is a snowy sea

In your eyes
my word is
a brilliant sun finished
the total solar eclipse.

변해가는 거리

늘 다니던 그 길에
미술관이 들어섰다
도시의 답답함이 체온을 상승시킬 때면
눈 감고 바람소리 듣던

머무는 내 마음을 모른 채
무시로 변해가는 거리
한 걸음 떨어진 내 기억은
미술관에 걸려
그 길을 걷고 있다.

A changing street

The way I used to go to and from
replaced an art museum
when the body temperature is elevated
by the stuffy feeling of the city,
I hear the sound of wind with my eyes shut

without knowing my mind to stay
a changing street any time
my memory one step separated
was walking the street
hanging the art gallery.

대지의 축복

The blessing of the earth

거북이 등에 오백 원

엄마 왜 거북이가 동전을 등에 업고 있어
아마도 장수를 기원하며 올려 둔 게지
모두 백 원인데 이 거북이는 왜 오백 원이야
그건 아마도 다섯 배나 더 오래 살고 싶은 게지
그럼 천 원을 올려 놓으면 천 년을 살 수 있어
그건 바람에 날아가 버려서
거북이가 약속을 지켜줄 수 없어

허망한 바램은 거북이도 어쩔 수 없구나
우린 동전을 올려 두지 말기로 하자.

Five hundred won on the back of tortoise

— Mom, why do the tortoise carry the coin on the back?
— maybe, the coin will be raised on the back
   in the sense of praying the longevity
— all is one hundred, but why this five hundred won?
— perhaps it'll be a wish to live five times longer
— if so, if one thousand is to be raised on it,
   will it be able to live longer as such?
— In that case, the tortoise can't keep a promise
   because of flying away in the wind

— Vain dream is unavoidable to a tortoise, too
   Let's not put the coin on it.

대지의 축복

비에 젖은 들판
시선마다 작품이 된다
마구 쏟아지는 비
음악이 된다

장마 후
개천에 시원스레 흐르는 물
삶의 역동적 심장 소리

이 순간을
느낄 수 있는 오감
희열이다.

The blessing of the earth

The field wet with the rain
becomes a work every eyes
pouring rain recklessly
becomes a music

After the rainy spell in summer
a brightly flowing water in the creek
a dynamic heart sound of life

Five senses
to feel this moment
it's a rapture.

단풍잎에 해가 걸리면

단풍잎에 해가 걸리면
서둘러 짐을 꾸린다
약속 없이 가는 너
한사코 보내기 싫어
추억이라는 페이지에
책갈피를 꽂아 둔다
얼기설기 쌓아 올린
고르지 못한 돌 단 사이
바람이 쉬어 간다

틈 조차 두지 않았더면
내 어찌 버텨냈겠는가.

When maple leaf is hung on the sun

when maple leaf is hung on the sun
I hastily make a bundle
you are going without promise
I really don't want to let you go
I put a bookmark
between the pages of memory
Between an uneven a stone step
accumulated in a disorderly way
The wind stops and starts

If it had no crevice,
how will I stick it out?

둥지를 떠나는 새

이른 아침
떠날 채비를 하는
한 마리 새
가장 높은 나뭇가지에 앉아
가장 예쁜 소리로
노래 한다

듣는 이
답하는 이 없어도
못내 아쉬운 이별 노래를 한다

떠날 수 없어서 둥지인 것을.

A bird leaving the nest

An early morning
a bird that is just prepared to leave
sings a song with the prettiest melody
sitting at the highest tree branches

Anyone is no hearing or answering
sings being deeply sorry to part someone.

Not leaving you, it's a nest.

드리운 건 낚시만은 아니다

물방개 톡톡 튀는 잔잔한 호수
살며시 드리운 건 낚시만은 아니다
간밤을 뒤척이게 하던 부엉이 울음
비에 젖어 어깨가 축 늘어진
아카시아 슬픈 잎새
그리고 나의 눈동자
출렁
월척을 기다린다

건져 올린 것은 잉어만은 아니다
드넓은 호수는
어머니의 가마솥이 되어
목마름
주림 없는
사랑까지 내어준다
호수 저편에서 들려오는
월척
가까이에서 볼 수 없는 들을 수 없는
그 소리.

What is hung down the water isn't a fish hook

A tranquil lake that a diving beetle
bounds with a snap
popping out and popping out
What is hung down the water silently
is not a fish hook
Owls hooting that made me ransack last night
a shoulder hung loosely wet with the rain
a sad leaf of an acacia
and the apple of the eye
I wait for a big fish lapping the lake

Pulling out of the water
is not only a carp
A broad lake
becoming a mother's cauldron
does a favor for thirst
even love without hunger
beyond the lake over there
catch a big fish!
the voice that can be seen or heard
in the neighborhood.

멈출 수 없다면

꽃인 줄 알았던
독버섯을 가슴에 키우며
물을 준다

커져가는 구멍
회오리 바람이 훑고 지난다
촛점을 잃은 불씨 하나
깜빡깜빡 졸며 별 헤는 밤

후 후
귓전의 숨소리
멈출 수 없다면
살을 파먹고라도
해독해야 할 공존.

If you can't stop

Raising the poisonous mushroom
mistaken for a flower in my heart
I spray water

the hole that gets bigger
the whirlwind drudges up
a live coal losing the focus
sleeping with a flash
the night counting the star

with puff after puff
breath sound of the ear rims
if you can't stop
in case of 'flesh—eating'
coexistence to detoxicate.

믿음

밤새 뒤척이는 몸짓에
참새도 잠을 이루지 못하는가
귀 기울여 들어보니
믿지 못해 뒤척이는 거란다

살아온 날이 허하여
병이 되었음을
탓하여 어디에 소용이 있을까

잔에 떨어지는 너의 눈망울
서둘러 촛불 밝힌다
너 오는 길.

A faith

Turning over the body at night
even sparrow passed a sleepless night
It's a sign of distrust
to listen carefully, they say

It is of no use to blame the vanity
and the pain of the past

Your eyeball falling into the glass
I light up a candlelight hurriedly
The way you are coming.

바람에 흔들리던
몇 날이 지나면

바람에 흔들리던
몇 날이 지나면
빨간 볼에 스치던
고추잠자리 날개도
굴곡이 선명한 허리선 휘감아 돌던
그
바람도
순수할 수밖에 없는
가을 하늘 아래
코스모스 물들여
보랏빛
사랑으로 남으리.

In a few days swaying with the wind

In passing a few days
swayed with the wind
even the wing of a red dragonfly
going pass by a red cheek
circumnutate a flection of waistline
and
the wind, too
under the autumn sky
of essence of purity
dyed a cosmos
will remain the violet love.

박꽃

달 보며 하얗게 피어나는
부끄러운 순정
무엇으로 지어 입은 드레스인지
화려함마저 감추는
순백의 순결
다소곳이 내민 그 입술에
머무는 꿀벌의
달콤한 애무.

A gourd flower

A shy naivety
blooming white looking at the moon
unknowable dress
a pure white innocence
concealed in a splendor
a sweet caress of
honeybee staying at lips
pushed out obediently.

촛불

눈 덮인 호수
홀로 춤추는 은반 위 발레리나
물결치는 머릿결 슬픈 목덜미
스미는 불빛에 반짝이는 백조

내가 태어난 날
불 밝힌 당신은
이미 알고 있었던가요
흔들리며 지탱하는 법을

차가운 얼음
온몸 밝혀 녹여 온 건가요.

A candle light

The lake covered with snow
a solo dancing ballerina on a silver plate
a sad nape with a waving hair
glittering swan filtered into the light

The day when I was born
you that lit the fire
are you aware of it?
how to sustain unsteadily

A cold ice
Have you been melted
with your body lightened?

시선

The eyes

친구와 나누는 반복되는 대화

2015년 7월 7일 소서
차창을 통해 쏟아지는 햇빛은 달갑지 않았다
한참 후에 걸려온 전화
언제나 그랬듯이 바쁘다
점심 먹자
그래
거기서 만나
어떻게 지내니
난 늘 그래
그래 넌 사막에서도 냉장고를 팔 수 있을 거야

난 늘 왜 사막에서 냉장고를 팔아야 하지
백사장을 아무 생각 없이 거닐면 내가 아닌 건가
잠시 생각에 빠져 본다
내 삶의 신선도를 지키기 위해 팔아 온 냉장고
신선도가 아닌 내 존재를 위해 오늘도 웃음으로 넘긴다
칼국수 냄비를 휘저어 공허한 배를 채우려는 순간
모시조개가 크게 입을 벌려 마주 웃어준다.

Repeated dialogue with a friend

In the year of 2015, July 7th
The sunshine gushing out through
the window was unwelcome
It is much later that there was a telephone call
It's very busy as usual
— Let's have a lunch
— oh, yes
— wait there
— how are you doing?
— so so
— Yes, you can sell the refrigerators
   even at the desert.

Why do I always have to sell
refrigerators at the desert?
if I stroll about the white beach
thoughtlessly, who on earth am I?
I fell into the thought for a moment
refrigerators on the market
to keep a degree of freshness of my life
I pass over with a smile for my existence
not a degree of freshness
a moment to appease my hunger
stirring a chopped noodles pan,
a shot-necked clam opens big and
makes a smile face to face.

하루를 왔다 가는 부레옥잠 꽃이 전하는 말

낮 기온 37도 불쾌지수 측정 불가
보송보송 따스했던 솜털 이불
바로 오늘이야
세탁기 돌아가는 소리
기분마저 상쾌하게 휙 던져 널고
철컥
뙤약볕에 남겨진 나
잔인한 휴일
약자의 강인함을 기어이 보여주고야 만다
꿈틀대는 악마를 잠재우고
물끄러미 바라본 부레옥잠
공작의 날개
가녀린 잎
화가의 상상력을 거부한 색채

내가 오늘 왔다 가는 것은
나의 부레가
가라 앉으려는 너의 멘탈의 부표이길 바라기 때문.

The word that water hyacinth of a day delivers

Temperature of blood heat, 37 degrees centigrade
discomfort index is unfairness of measurement
This is the very day!
the sound of rolling a washing machine
putting a pleasant mood into it with a jerk
I was under the scorching sun with a snap

A cruel holiday
toughness of the weak is to be exposed
by all means
I put to sleep a devil giving a wiggle
a water hyacinth looked at blankly

The wings of peacock
a slender leaves
colors refused artist's imagination

What I come and go today
is a wish that my bladder would be your
mental buoy going to sink down

생명의 탄생

감미로운 음악
내 심장이 가장 활발히 뛸 때
들려오는 목소리
취하는 건 코끝에 스치는 감동
그리고 너

무아의 세계에서 들려오는
새벽의 초침
내 눈동자에 이는 파도

일생을 두고 탄생할
인고의 의미.

The birth of life

A sweet melody
when my heart begins to beat extremely
a voice to be heard
what is fascinated
is an emotion
touching the tip of a nose
and you

the second hand of a dawn
from the self—renunciation
waves stirring my pupil

a life of patient endurance
to be born through till death.

시상

만리포 백사장을 다 걸어도
떠오르지 않는 너
미친 듯 바닷물을 들이 마셔도
채워지지 않는 너
가슴이 불러도
다가오지 않는 너

불 꺼진 텅 빈 방
지독한 고독의 독주를 마시고서야
가슴에 안기는 너.

A poetic sentiment

Walking a Malipo white beach all through
you have not begun to stir in me
though I drank up seawater in a frenzy
you won't fill me
even if I want you in my heart,
you don't come near to me

An unlighted, empty room
and then only
you want to be embraced
after drinking a strong liquor

시선

내가 향하는 곳은
밝은
선명한
시들지 않는
나의 색을 잃지 않을

오직
나의 캔버스.

The eyes

The place where I headed for
is a bright
obvious
unwithered
not losing my own color

exclusively
my canvas.

시작

함께 가면 안주한다
혼자 가면 포기한다
혼자 출발해서 좋은 길동무를 얻으면
함께 도착할 수 있다

좋은 길동무를 얻으면.

The beginning

If you go together, you live in comfort
if you go alone, you give up
even if you start alone at first,
if you can get a good companion,
You can reach the goal together

if you have a good traveller.

알 수 없는 새

천둥 번개 태풍이 지나가면
폭염도 싫지만은 않다

이른 아침이면 어느새 창가에 들어
조로롱
조로롱
이름이 뭐냐 묻지 않았지
맑은 노래만 들려주고 홀연히 떠난 너
새삼 이 밤
너의 목소리가 들려온다
하릴없이 끄적이는 이 밤을
버릴 수 없어
널 기다린다
조로롱
조로롱.

An unknowable bird

If thunder, lightning and typhoon
passes by, even summer heat
isn't disagreeable

when I sit at the window
in the early morning
zororong zororong
I didn't ask, what's your name?
but you flew away abruptly
after singing a clear song
At this night
your voice is being heard
you don't quit doodling helplessly
I'm waiting for you
Zororong Zororong.

야생화

이름도 없이
붉지도 않게
피었어도

뽀얀 분칠 단장하고
아침을 기다리는

분명
나
꽃이랍니다.

A wildflower

Though it blooms
without being nameless
and with no red

making up face
with a creamy powder
waits for the morning

Of course
I am
Flower.

열정이 되는 추억

텅 빈 의자는 주인을 기다린다
텅 빈 마음은 그날을 더듬는다
추억이라는 기름진 퇴비는
오늘을 풍족히 하고
내일의 가르침이 된다
해서
한 고비 한 순간도
나는 열정을 바친다.

The memory becoming the passion

An empty chair waits for its owner
an empty mind looks back upon the day

A fertile manure of the memory
makes today be abundant
becomes the teaching of tomorrow
therefore,
even one crisis and moment
I devote a enthusiasm.

오늘이 그리운 날이 곧 온다

언젠가의 그날이 그리운 것처럼
오늘이 그리운 날이 곧 온다

머지않아 오늘이 오더라도
후회는 하지 말자
매일 시작되는 무모한 삶의 도전
그로 인해 매일 새롭게 태어나는 나

오늘이 그립더라도
내일의 나는
안나푸르나를 정복할 것이다.

The day comes to long for today

As we long for the day of someday
The day comes to long for today

Though today comes before long
let's not regret
the challenge of a reckless life
that begins everyday
for the reason like that
I will be born anew everyday

Though I long for today
'I' of tomorrow
will conquer the Annapurna.

용서의 시간

The time of forgiveness

나를 닮은 솔방울

활짝 웃는다
빈 껍데기인 채로

층층이 담을 쌓아
품었던 씨앗을 날려 보내고
버틸 힘조차 없어
낙엽 위로
툭.

A pinecone resembled me

It smiles brightly
with an empty shell

It piled the wall by layers
and had an embraced seed fly
without sustaining power
on the fallen leaves
with a pat.

오래된 사진

주섬주섬 가버리는 시간들
기록은 기억을 찾아준다
멀어져 간 과거들을
곁에 머물게 하는 건
기록 뿐이다.

An aged photograph

Times going away one by one
documents recover the memory
what made pasts faded away stay at hand
is nothing but the record.

용서의 시간

귓전에 맴도는 슬픈 노래가
잊혀져 가는 널 다시 데려다 놓는다

가파른 시계바늘이
째깍째깍 울부짖으며 종용하는
자유
변질된 뇌세포의 치유

수화기를 집어 든다
더 늦기 전에.

The time of forgiveness

The sad song spinning round the ear rims
brings you again that became forgotten

A steep hands of a clock
lets out a howl quickly
composing the freedom

a healing of brain cell
changed in quality

I pick up a receiver
before it's too late.

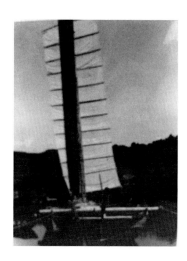

정동진 백사장

끝없이 펼쳐진
하얀 도화지 위로
비 개인 하늘이 시리다

하늘을 삼켜버린
그 바다에
도화지를 담근다

알록달록한 내 욕심은
황홀한 수채화를 그려낸다

파란 머릿속
한 점 뭉게구름
날개를 펼쳐
선명하게 써주는

너의 선택을 믿어라.

A Jeongdongjin white beach

On the white drawing paper
spreaded endlessly
a clear sky is chilly

I dip a drawing paper
into the sea swallowed the sky

my mottled desire
draws a fantastic water color

In the blue brain
a piece of cumulus spread the wings
and write down vividly

Rely on your choice.

파도는 그 어떤 것도

그 어떤 것도 의도하지 않는 파도
부서지고서야 바다에 빠진 걸 알았을까
희뿌연 안개비가 주는 이른 아침의 여운

맞설 수 조차 없이 부서져
천국인지 지옥인지 모를
벼랑 끝의 전율
한사코 움켜쥔 실낱같은
이미 버려진 욕심

헝클어진 시간을 빗어
밀려나간 바다를 바란다
이른 아침 안개의 모습으로 오는.

The waves is anything more

Not even face against the waves
they were breaking into pieces
without knowing heaven or the hell

The wave that not intended anything
It doesn't know that fell into the sea
until it was broken
a lingering mood of a faint drizzle
in the early morning

A thrill at the cliff
already forsaken desire
grasped desperately
hanging by a thread

Combing a tangled time
I expect a rushing waves of the sea
coming the figure of fog
soon in morning.

편견

가끔 나는 귀가 들리지 않는다
가끔 나는 눈이 보이지 않는다

그래야
살 수 있다 하니

치료를 포기할 생각이다.

A prejudice

Sometimes I'm inaudible
sometimes I'm invisible

Only so
I can survive, they say

I'm intended to abandon the cure.

하지 말았어야 할 염려

만남과 이별을 반복하며
잊고도 살아갈 수 있게 해주는 것을
잠 못 이루는 몇 날 몇 밤
채 이별준비가 되기도 전에
문 두드리는 너
환희
이 말밖에

너를 처음 만난 날 전부라고 생각했다
니가 떠날 준비를 할 즈음
어느 날 불쑥 내밀어진 손
다시 미소가 드리우고
다시 새긴다
뇌이며 살 수 있을 만큼.

You should not have been anxious

Repeating a meeting and parting
I can live even forgetting you
several days of a sleepless night
before preparing the farewell as yet
you knocking the door
a rapture
nothing but the word

The day when I saw you for the first time
I thought that you mean everything to me
at the time of preparation for separating
you reached out your hand abruptly
casting a smile again
and I carved in my mind
As such to repeat myself.

화도에서 환원되는 나

치워
허리나 펴고 앉게

넓게만 보이던 고구마 밭 한가운데 그 바위는
나만의 섬이었고
어머니를 치유하는 매트리스였다
자칫 깎아버리고 쪼개어버린 내 조각들을
화도의 *너렁바위에 다시 모아
머언 발치로 나를 바라보는
널 맞이할 시간으로의 환원

버거운 정오의 볕
정수리를 타고 흐르는
땀방울 훔치며
꽃잎 밥상 차리는
철없는 나에게
쏘아 붙인 어머니의 한 마디.

*너렁바위 : 넓고 납작한 바위

Restored to myself in Hwado

Throw away
I'll sit stretching my back

the rock in the midst of sweet potato fields
that looked spacious
was my own island and mattress
to cure my mother
cutting and splitting pieces
I recollected them
at the Neorung rock of Hwado
and I was reduced to the time
to meet you at a distant place

A sunshine of the noon
that is beyond my capacity
wiping beads of sweat
flowing through the crown of the head
mother jerked out a piece of word
for my thoughtlessness
setting a dining table of petals.

* Neorung rock: broad and flat rock

95

입술로 다가오는 연잎 향기

매끄러운 몸매
면사포로 향을 가린
다소곳한 홍매빛 얼굴
미끄러져 입술로 스민다

한겨울 언 손
호호 불어주던
너의 입술이
이처럼 달콤했던가.

A scent of a lotus leaf
approaching the lips

A smooth figure
an obedient red plum blossom's face
concealed the smell with a bridal veil
soaks into the lips

Hands frozen stiff all winter
you would breathe upon my hands
to keep them warm
what a sweet lips you are!

보여지는 것과 보는 것

너울거리는 여신의 치마폭이 여명에 물들면
궁전 근위대는 어느새 틈 하나 주지 않고
각기 대형을 갖추어 성을 호위한다

하늘로 제물을 나르는 크레인
우러르지 못하는 병정들
허리 굽혀 제를 올릴 새
기울어가는 하루

그렇다
건설의 현장은 노역의 현장이 아닌
비바람으로 다지고 달빛에 공양하는
영혼을 쏟아내어 빚어올리는 혼의 성전

마침내 천 일의 기도가 끝이 나면
쏟아놓았던 영혼들을 주섬주섬 챙길 것이다
그제서라도 웃어준다면 이대로 남아도 좋다
그 천 일 동안
하나의 톱니바퀴로.

To be seen and to see

If the width of joined parts in a skirt of Goddess
is dyed with a daybreak
the Royal Guards of a palace guard the castle
without making a gap so soon
in good formation.

a crane carrying a sacrifice to the heaven
soldiers that fail to look up to
raising the ceremony bending the body
a day that is declining.

Yes,
construction site is not a labor house
but the sanctuary of the spirit
resulted from the soul that provided for
moonlight hardened with the rain and wind

In the end
If thousand day's prayer is over
I'll get souls devoted in order one by one
if you smile then, I may as well remain as it is
for thousand days
with a toothed wheel.

사랑 다이어트

안개주의보
시야를 가린 거리의 질주
고장난 브레이크
젖어드는 온몸의 무게
조여오는 심장

사랑 다이어트를 시작할 시간

흐드러진 단풍
국화꽃 내음에 맺히는 이슬
반쯤 누워 무관심한 초승달
아이러니의 *카타르

사랑의 다이어트 필요한 시간

*Catarrh : 감기 등으로 코와 목의
점막에 생기는 염증

Love diet

An advisory for fog
a scamper of street blocking my view
the malfunction of a brake
a weight of the whole body that gets wet
a compressing heart

the time to begin a love diet

A red leaves in full glory
dewy chrysanthemum scent
an indifferent crescent moon
the catarrh of an irony

It's time to have a love diet.

후 기

하나의 작품을 탄생시키는 일, 참 어렵고 조심스럽다.

미국 이민을 떠나는 시점에서 사랑하는 내 나라와 사랑하는 사람들과의 물리적 이별 앞에 놓치고 싶지 않은 기억들을 찾아 여행하는 마음으로 이 책을 쓰기 시작했다.

그렇기 때문에 소심해지기도 했고 그렇기 때문에 욕심을 부리기도 했던 것 같다. 과분한 행복에 눈물을 흘린 기억도 있지만 그 눈물은 더 큰 용기가 되어 힘을 실어 주었다.

새로운 시작 앞에 나의 다짐이기도 한 아래 두 편의 작품을 다시 되짚어 보면서 아쉬움과 희망이 공존했기에 더 많은 것을 얻을 수도, 더 많은 것을 비울 수도 있었던 이 여행을 마무리하고자 한다.

안개주의보
시야를 가린 거리의 질주
고장난 브레이크
젖어드는 온몸의 무게
조여오는 심장

사랑 다이어트를 시작할 시간

흐드러진 단풍
국화꽃 내음에 맺히는 이슬
반쯤 누워 무관심한 초승달
아이러니의 카타르

사랑의 다이어트 필요한 시간

－〈사랑 다이어트 전문〉

고독이라는 지독한 단어 앞에 어느 누가 당당할 수 있을까. 가끔 일부러 눈을 가리고 무모한 질주를 한다. 고독해야

자신의 깊은 내면과 소통할 수 있는 반면 고독이 외로움이
되기도 하는 아이러니로부터 나 자신을 다시 점검해 나가는
다짐이기도 하다.

> 파랑새를 띄워 보낸 저 너머
> 저벅저벅 다가오는 약속의 시간
> 두려움이란 놈은 언제나
> 자신감을 앞서 걷는다
>
> 독백만이 걸음을 재촉한다
> 꽃으로 대답하는 한 줄기 칡 넝쿨
> 아무 때고 반겨주는 해묵은 갈색 의자
> 힘든 하루를 삼켜버리고
> 피를 토하는 붉은 노을
> 심장에 새겨 두고
> 앞선 두려움 제쳐 걷는다
>
> 보내는 이 없음에.
>
> －〈詩作하는 旅者 始作하는 女子 전문〉

　누구나 새로운 도전 앞에서 두려움을 갖는 것은 당연한
일일 것이다. 그러나 두려움을 이겨내야만 첫 발걸음을 내
디딜 수가 있다. 두려움에 밀리는 순간 나를 위로할 핑계를
찾는다.
　누구 때문에, 무엇 때문에, 그것 때문에….
　그러나 보내는 이도 붙잡는 이도 없는 것이 자신의 내면
인 것이다. 시를 쓰지 않으면 작품이 될 수 없고, 가 보지
않으면 정상에 설 수 없다.

　그래서 詩作하고 그래서 始作한다.